I LOVE YOU, PLANET

By Emily Dougherty

Illustrations by Katie Vander Velden

Copyright 2020

With a home comes lots of tasks
This I'm told by Mom

Dusting, scrubbing, sweeping
The list goes on and on

Just like my house, dear Planet
You're better when you're clean

So to you I make a promise
To keep you bright and green

Your grassy hills and fields
Give me the perfect place

To watch the white stars sparkle

Deep in outer space

So every time I walk or bike
I'm showing that I care

Dad and I can plant some seeds
And wait for them to grow

So when I'm big and tall
I'll have a tree to show!

Your oceans run for miles
Mysterious and blue

They're home to many creatures
As unique as me and you!

These seas offer endless views
With shades of blue and teal

Our garbage has no place there
Clean oceans are ideal

To keep you healthy, Planet
And maintain your natural beauty

Walking is so good for me
And planting trees is fun

These are both easy ways
To protect the place I love

I will do my very best
To not let it go to waste

When I reduce, reuse, recycle
You, Planet, I can save!